PEOPLE IN THE NEWS

Justin Timberlake

Musical Megastar

By Nicole Horning

Portions of this book originally appeared in *Justin Timberlake* by Terri Dougherty.

LUCENT PRESS

Published in 2020 by
Lucent Press, an Imprint of Greenhaven Publishing, LLC
353 3rd Avenue
Suite 255
New York, NY 10010

Designer: Deanna Paternostro
Editor: Nicole Horning

Library of Congress Cataloging-in-Publication Data

Names: Horning, Nicole, author.
Title: Justin Timberlake : musical megastar / Nicole Horning.
Description: First edition. | New York : Lucent Press, 2020. | Series: People in the news | Includes bibliographical references and index. | Audience: Ages 12 | Audience: Grades 7-9
Identifiers: LCCN 2019030127 (print) | LCCN 2019030128 (ebook) | ISBN 9781534568389 (library binding) | ISBN 9781534568372 (paperback) | ISBN 9781534568396 (ebook)
Subjects: LCSH: Timberlake, Justin, 1981—Juvenile literature. | Rock musicians–United States–Biography–Juvenile literature.
Classification: LCC ML3930.T58 H67 2020 (print) | LCC ML3930.T58 (ebook) | DDC 782.42164092 [B]–dc23
LC record available at https://lccn.loc.gov/2019030127
LC ebook record available at https://lccn.loc.gov/2019030128

Printed in China

CPSIA compliance information: Batch #BW20KL: For further information contact Greenhaven Publishing LLC, New York, New York, at 1-844-317-7404.

Contents

Foreword

We live in a world where the latest news is always available and where it seems we have unlimited access to the lives of the people in the news. Entire television networks are devoted to news about politics, sports, and entertainment. Social media has allowed people to have an unprecedented level of interaction with celebrities. We have more information at our fingertips than ever before. However, how much do we really know about the people we see on television news programs, social media feeds, and magazine covers?

Despite the constant stream of news, the full stories behind the lives of some of the world's most newsworthy men and women are often unknown. Who was Lady Gaga before she became a star? What does LeBron James do when he is not playing basketball? What inspires Lin-Manuel Miranda?

This series aims to answer questions like these about some of the biggest names in pop culture, sports, politics, and technology. While the subjects of this series come from all walks of life and areas of expertise, they share a common magnetism that has made them all captivating figures in the public eye. They have shaped the world in some unique way, and—in many cases—they are poised to continue to shape the world for many years to come.

These biographies are not just a collection of basic facts. They tell compelling stories that show how each figure grew to become a powerful public personality. Each book aims to paint a complete, realistic picture of its subject—from the challenges they overcame to the controversies they caused. In doing so, each book reinforces the idea that even the most famous faces on the news are real people who are much more complex than we are often shown in brief video clips or sound bites. Readers are also reminded that there is even more to a person than what they present to the world through social media posts, press releases, and interviews. The whole story of a person's life can only be discovered by digging beneath the surface of their public persona, and that is what this series allows readers to do.

The books in this series are filled with enlightening quotes from speeches and interviews given by the subjects, as well as quotes and anecdotes from those who know their story best: family, friends, coaches, and colleagues. All quotes are noted to provide guidance for further research. Detailed lists of additional resources are also included, as are timelines, indexes, and unique photographs. These text features come together to enhance the reading experience and encourage readers to dive deeper into the stories of these influential men and women.

Fame can be fleeting, but the subjects featured in this series have real staying power. They have fundamentally impacted their respective fields and have achieved great success through hard work and true talent. They are men and women defined by their accomplishments, and they are often seen as role models for the next generation. They have left their mark on the world in a major way, and their stories are meant to inspire readers to leave their mark, too.

Introduction

Justified

Justin Timberlake is an incredibly talented performer. When fans walk into an arena where he is performing, they know that Timberlake is not merely going to step on the stage and sing their favorite songs. He is going to completely entertain them. Timberlake's live shows typically involve a massive stage set, dancing, and plenty of interaction with the audience. However, long before he was performing songs such as "Can't Stop the Feeling!," "TKO," and "Mirrors" for packed arenas, Timberlake was a Mouseketeer on *The All New Mickey Mouse Club* and then was widely adored by millions of fans as a member of *NSYNC.

Young Man

Music was an important part of Justin Timberlake's life from an early age. He sang in the church choir as a child, and some members of his family were musicians. His uncle was in a bluegrass band, and his grandfather had played guitar with the famous singer Elvis Presley. Justin was raised around a wide variety of music, and this influence would show up later in his career. His father introduced him to bands such as Queen, and he was also introduced to artists such as B. B. King because Memphis, Tennessee—the city Justin calls home—was the home of the blues.

Justin's musical upbringing and talent started to become apparent when he was quite young. Long before shows such as *American Idol*, there was *Star Search*. *Star Search* ran from 1983 to 1995 and then briefly came back in 2003 to 2004, and it was a talent competition show like *American Idol* and *The Voice*. In 1992, 11-year-old Justin auditioned on the show and lost. This loss did not stop him from pursuing his dream, however. In 1993 and 1994, Justin starred on the comedic variety show *The All New Mickey Mouse Club* (frequently known as *MMC*). *MMC* also featured other pop stars and actors who would be famous in the future, including JC Chasez, who would join Justin as a member of *NSYNC.

In 1995, a group was forming in Orlando, Florida. Lou Pearlman, manager of the Backstreet Boys, wanted to create another boy band. He saw Chris Kirkpatrick singing in a show at Universal Studios Florida and approached him about putting together a music group. As Justin was well known from his work on *MMC*, his mother received news that a group was forming and she put together an audition tape for Justin. He was added into the boy band and then suggested former *MMC* costar JC Chasez. Joey Fatone and Lance Bass joined shortly after. JC and Joey were friends, and Joey and Chris knew each other because they both worked at Universal Studios. Lance was added to the band based on a recommendation from Justin's vocal coach. With this final addition, *NSYNC was formed.

*NSYNC got their start in Europe before gathering fame in the United States. This formula previously worked for the Backstreet Boys, so it was used for *NSYNC as well. The band's first album was released in Europe, and the band did promotional tours in Europe before their album was released in the United States in March 1998. The album did not take off well in the United States until the Backstreet Boys were not able to do a Disney Channel concert special. *NSYNC was called in to fill their place, and

*NSYNC was formed in the mid-1990s and released their first album in 1998. From front to back, Lance Bass, Justin Timberlake, Joey Fatone, Chris Kirkpatrick, and JC Chasez are shown here.

the album that had debuted at number 82 on the Billboard charts soared up to number 2. The album sold 10 million copies just in the United States. The band went on to release a Christmas album, *Home for Christmas*, that same year. Their next album, *No Strings Attached*, was released in 2000, followed by what would be their last album, *Celebrity*, in 2001. Around this time, Justin Timberlake decided that he wanted to leave the band and pursue a solo career. The move was portrayed as a break from the band, and many fans hoped to see them reunite. However, as of summer 2019, Timberlake's move has been a permanent one, and the band has not reunited except to perform a few songs on MTV award shows and at the Coachella music festival.

Giving Fans What They Want

Justin Timberlake's solo debut album, *Justified*, was released in 2002. The album had several hits, such as "Cry Me a River," "Like I Love You," "Rock Your Body," and "Señorita." These songs were massive hits and remain fan favorites even years after the album was released, and Timberlake continues to sing them on tours, such as the 2018 and 2019 Man of the Woods Tour. Timberlake's follow-up to *Justified* did not arrive until 2006 with *FutureSex/LoveSounds*. During the gap between albums, Timberlake started his acting career in movies such as *Alpha Dog* and recovered from the heavy touring schedule he had been doing for years. *FutureSex/LoveSounds* debuted an entirely new sound for Timberlake that critics praised. *Rolling Stone* stated in 2016 that Timberlake

> *destroyed any doubt of his artistry or potential with the mature, innovative* FutureSex/LoveSounds. *For his second post-boy-band solo outing, the pop star experimented with R&B, funk and rock to create a piece of music well ahead of its time. Today, the LP's influence can still be heard in everything from the worldly electro-soul of Zayn Malik to the moody sound of newcomers like Bryson Tiller. The album also signaled Timberlake's transition from pop hitmaker and Hollywood It Boy to a legitimate force as a musician and actor.*[1]

Timberlake is shown here performing at the 2018 Super Bowl halftime show. His album *Man of the Woods* was also released around this time, and he opened the show with the song "Filthy" from the album.

Timberlake continued to act in movies, such as *The Social Network*, *Friends with Benefits*, and *In Time*, while fans speculated about where his musical career was going. While the gap between his first and second solo albums was four years, it ended up being seven years between *FutureSex/LoveSounds* and the 2013 albums *The 20/20 Experience*, which were released in two parts with the second one being released six months after the first. Many fans felt the wait for these albums was worth it. The songs were recorded with Timbaland, and Timberlake experimented with new sounds throughout the albums. Songs such as "Mirrors" and "Suit and Tie," which also featured JAY-Z, catapulted the albums to the top of the Billboard charts. The first album sold around 1 million copies in the first week of release.

Timberlake continued to prove himself as a legitimate force in music, and in 2018, he performed at the Super Bowl halftime show as the solo headliner. Around this time, he also released the long-awaited album *Man of the Woods*.

Justin Timberlake and Jessica Biel are shown here at the Golden Globe Awards in 2018. The couple married in 2012 after dating for around five years.

Timberlake grew from a *Star Search* contestant who lost to a Mouseketeer to a member of a popular boy band. While many were thinking that boy bands were just a brief trend and the names of their members would be forgotten soon, Timberlake proved them all wrong. He became a widely respected musician and actor, and while he was working on that, he also became a husband to actress Jessica Biel, father, and author.

Chapter One

Tennessee Kid

Justin Timberlake grew up around Memphis, Tennessee, which is known for its musical culture. Blues music developed in this area, Elvis Presley's home was in the city, and Justin grew up in a musical family. The makings for a pop star who would take the world by storm were all there. Luckily, his family recognized the amount of talent that Justin had at a young age and also what that talent could grow into. His ear for music showed itself at an astoundingly young age—at only a few months old, he would move his legs to the beat of the music that his mother, Lynn, was playing. She said, "We'd change the music and he'd kick his legs to the new beat … We'd say to our friends, 'Dude! Look at this!' He was like a little toy."[2] Justin's talent could not be denied—when he was just around two years old, he was singing along with songs on the radio.

Talented Child

Justin Timberlake was born on January 31, 1981, to Randy and Lynn Timberlake. Lynn had Justin when she was young herself—she was only 20 years old. When Justin was three years old, Randy and Lynn divorced. Both parents remained

Importance of Family

Although he began performing at a young age, Justin Timberlake always remained close to his family. He called his grandmother, Sadie Bomar, whenever he was coming home to Tennessee, telling her not to forget to make his favorite peach cobbler. She even brought him a batch when he was touring with *NSYNC in 2000. Timberlake is especially close to his mother, and both of them have stated that they grew up together because Lynn was so young when she had Justin.

Timberlake is shown here with his mother, Lynn. His family is important to him, and they often attend events with him, such as the one shown here.

close to Justin after the divorce, and he developed an especially strong bond with his mother. Lynn remarried banker Paul Harless when Justin was five. Justin got along well with his stepfather. Justin's father also remarried and had two sons—Jonathan and Stephen—with his new wife.

Justin grew up in Millington, Tennessee, one of the main suburbs of Memphis. While he had a feel for music, as a young child he did not go out of his way to put on shows or entertain people around him. His mother described him as a quiet boy, who would walk around with his head down.

Music was all around Justin as he was growing up. He listened to country music on the radio and learned about singers such as Johnny Cash and Willie Nelson from his grandfather. He overcame his shyness to sing in the church gospel choir, and his grandfather also taught him the basics of playing guitar.

Lynn recognized Justin's singing ability and thought her son had the potential to be a star. She encouraged her shy child to use his talent onstage and entered him in talent shows. He began performing under the name Justin Randall, and he sang mainly country and gospel music because audiences seemed most interested in these music styles.

At age eight, Justin began taking voice lessons. His superior vocal talent and knack for performing soon became apparent to his classmates. When he was in third grade at E. E. Jeter Elementary School, he sang as the warm-up act for a lip-synching contest and impressed the audience. He was so good at the New Kids on the Block song he performed that girls mobbed him. "It was like something out of a Beatles movie," recalled Paul Harless. "They had him pinned up against a wall. Some wanted to get his autograph. Some tried to give him money."[3]

Expanding Musical Tastes

The many adoring young fans did not scare Justin away from music or performing. The more he learned about music, the more intrigued he became. He spent his time learning about

Justin is shown here at a recording session in 1992. A record executive saw him perform at a talent show and was so impressed that he asked Justin to record a song.

different styles and sounds and the layering of harmonies. At age 11, he was introduced to the blues and became interested in learning about its roots. In addition, he began to appreciate the rhythm and blues (R&B) music of singers and musicians such as Al Green, Stevie Wonder, and Marvin Gaye.

His father's music collection also expanded his musical tastes. Randy Timberlake would play the Eagles and Bob Seger when Justin visited him. Justin also became interested in the harmonies of the rock group Queen and was so taken by the song "Bohemian Rhapsody" that he would lock himself in his room and listen carefully to the music and harmony, trying to learn every nuance.

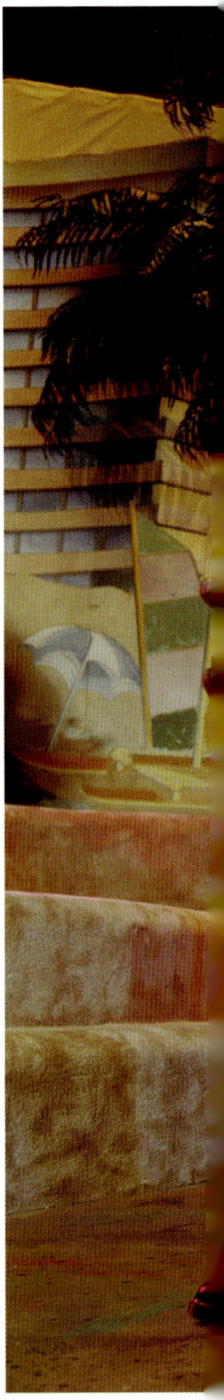

Singing Competitions

No longer shy about his vocal talent, Justin did not hesitate to show what he could do when his mom entered him in a number of talent shows. These shows allowed him to polish his singing talent and gain experience as a performer. Justin was learning to be comfortable onstage impressing an audience.

In 1992, at age 11, he expanded his career and entered the realm of television with a tryout for the *Star Search* talent show. *Star Search* was much like *American Idol* or *The Voice* is today. Contestants performed in front of a panel of judges for the chance to be on television and win a prize for their talent. Dressed in a cowboy hat and western shirt, Justin passed the audition and made it to the televisied round as a contestant. However, the show's judges did not choose him as a winner when he performed on the show.

MMC

The show helped the young performer attract notice, however, and further expand his singing career. In 1993, he was selected to be part of *The All New Mickey Mouse Club*, or *MMC*. He and his mother moved to Orlando, Florida, where the show was produced. The 12-year-old left behind his home, friends, and ordinary life in Memphis for a chance to be part of a nationally televised show.

MMC was based on a similar series that was popular in the 1950s and had also been remade in the 1970s. The show brought together a number of talented young singers and dancers and had them perform songs, dances, and short sketches. The show was packed with talent: Britney

In addition to Justin (top right), the cast of *MMC* included Christina Aguilera (middle right), Britney Spears (bottom right), and Ryan Gosling (bottom left).

Spears, Christina Aguilera, Ryan Gosling, JC Chasez, and Keri Russell were all part of the show.

Justin's selection as a member of the show's cast changed his life. Before, he had been an average student and a member of the school's basketball team who spent some of his free time performing in talent shows. As a Mouseketeer, performing would be the main focus of his life.

Justin was on the show for almost two years. He spent a significant amount of time learning the songs, dance moves, and comedy sketches that were part of the show, but he also enjoyed a number of perks as a cast member.

Justin had the opportunity to follow in the footsteps of his musical idol, Michael Jackson, who had also begun his career as a young singer. *MMC* gave Justin a chance to learn more about singing and dancing and to perform onstage before a live audience. Justin began to appreciate what it was like to be in the spotlight.

In one of the show's concert segments, Justin and Britney Spears did a duet of the song "I Feel for You." He commanded attention onstage yet easily shared the spotlight with Britney.

"The Earring Song"

At age 13, Justin begged his parents to let him get his ear pierced. All his friends had earrings, he reasoned, and he should have one, too. His stepfather made Justin earn it rather than simply giving in to his request. If Justin wrote a song and sang it at a family gathering, he could have his ear pierced, his stepfather said.

Justin really wanted that earring, so he wrote "The Earring Song" and sang it to his parents and a friend while they were on vacation. His stepfather kept his word. When they returned to Memphis, Justin got his earring.

Justin was not always the star of the show, however. He had his share of moments onstage, but he also sang backup for the other performers. He learned how to perform as part of a group, not just as the center of attention.

In addition to song and dance routines, the show also featured profiles of the young actors in the cast. Justin introduced kids to Memphis, the city where he grew up. He proudly showed off its trolleys, the amphitheater where he saw concerts, and Elvis's home at Graceland. He also showed his humorous side as he played golf and told kids that the key to a good putt was to put the ball in the hole.

Justin stayed close to a number of his friends from Memphis even though he had moved to Orlando. He brought several of them onto the show with him for his profile segment. Viewers got a look into a natural and funny side of his personality as he and his friends did Elvis impersonations. Justin also toured the city with his friends, looking relaxed in front of the camera. It was not the city's attractions but its serenity that Justin said he liked.

*Beginning of *NSYNC*

Justin had a group of close friends and a fun job as a performer, but he still had to deal with the problems faced by many young teens. Justin had acne and was called names such as "Pizza Face." His curly hair was difficult to manage. "I used to get picked on all the time," he said. "I had terrible acne, weird hair. My arms were too long."[4]

MMC was canceled in 1995; Disney stopped making new episodes. That same year, however, manager Lou Pearlman was looking to form another boy band. He had already had success with the Backstreet Boys, who were becoming more popular each day, and he wanted to see if that success could strike again. Around this time, he watched a musical group perform at the Universal Studios Florida theme park and was interested in one of the group members, Chris Kirkpatrick. Pearlman stated that he would provide the financing for the band if Chris could find the members for it.

Because Justin had been popular on *MMC*, he was well known in the Orlando area and Lynn got a call about a group forming in Florida. She helped put an audition tape together, and Justin was added to the group. Justin then suggested JC Chasez as a third member. Joey Fatone was the fourth member to join the boy band, and he had connections with both JC

*NSYNC formed in 1995 and quickly became massively popular. The band members are shown here with Lou Pearlman less than a year after the band formed.

and Chris. Joey performed at Universal Studios Florida in the Beetlejuice show, so he knew Chris from working in the same park. He was also an early friend of JC's when JC moved to Florida to work on *MMC*.

The addition of the fifth member was more complicated. The fifth member needed to be a bass singer. Joey recommended a friend of his named Jason, and he was added to the group—until he had to sign the contract. He decided not to join the group after all because he did not like the musical direction of the group.

Finding someone to replace Jason proved difficult, and the group had to perform at a showcase in just a few weeks. They contacted Justin's vocal coach, who recommended Lance Bass. Because Lance was still in high school in his junior year, his mom was hesitant to let him join the band. However, eventually, Lance flew down to Orlando. October 1, 1995, was the official start date of the group, who got their name—*NSYNC—because of how synchronized they sounded when singing together. The musical talents of these five singers put together would make them a force in the music industry and tough competition for other groups such as the Backstreet Boys.

Chapter Two

Tearin' Up Fans' Hearts

Justin was only 14 years old when he joined *NSYNC. The other members were not much older. JC was 19, Joey was 18, Lance was 16, and Chris was the oldest at 23. The young ages of the band members did not mean that they were not serious about their music careers, however. The group put a lot of time and effort into building their fan base and then maintaining it. They started in Europe, and in 1998, they came back to the United States, where they were a musical force to be reckoned with. However, while they were driving fans crazy at the beginning of their career, by 2002, they were tearing up fans' hearts for a completely different reason when they went on a hiatus that proved to be permanent.

The Europe Tactic

*NSYNC's manager, Lou Pearlman, wanted the group to build a following in Europe before releasing their record in the United States. The sugary pop sound that would be the hallmark of the group's first hits was popular in European dance clubs, so *NSYNC traveled to Stockholm, Sweden, to record their first song. Bass stated, "Lou [Pearlman] promised us, 'Oh yeah, your song will be released before the Backstreet Boys,'

*NSYNC is shown here in 1998. Their first album was released that year in the United States, and the group finally made their way back home to tour.

and of course that was a lie. So I was very aware that the first group out in America was going to take the whole market."[5]

Studio time was expensive, so the group members were serious about making the most of their recording time. Timberlake and the others had to work both diligently and quickly to produce quality tracks on time. The song "I Want You Back" was expected to take the group four days to record, but they did it in one.

They still took the time to blend their voices on each track to bring out their best vocal qualities. On tracks such as "Sailing," a song first made popular by Christopher Cross in the 1980s, they carefully layered their voices to bring out the nuances of the music. "We layered that song until I don't think you could add any more harmony," Timberlake said. "We did as much with our voices as we could."[6]

The resulting album, titled **NSYNC*, led with "Tearin' Up My Heart" and included the popular songs "Here We Go," "Thinking of You (I Drive Myself Crazy)," and "I Want You Back."

Putting Together the First Tour

To promote the album, the group made videos and prepared to tour in Europe. They planned stops in Germany, Austria, and Switzerland. Before the tour, however, the group needed to put together a show. In addition to singing, the boys rehearsed dance routines that had them doing hip-hop dance moves in unison. Their synchronized dancing became part of the group's trademark and their appeal. In order to get the routines perfect, they had to put in hours of practice, sometimes in uncomfortable conditions. They rehearsed in an old warehouse that was not air conditioned, and a great deal of sweat went into getting everything perfect. They were hopping around in the heat for 3 or 4 hours 4 times a week, and although it was uncomfortable, it gave them the strength they would need for an intense tour schedule.

Their hard work paid off when they appeared onstage. The audience appreciated not only their music but their dancing as well. They were able to connect with the crowd and keep audiences entertained. *NSYNC was soon booked for television appearances on European channels and a sold out 17-city tour in Germany. Their popularity increased as they were featured in teen magazines. They quickly became so well known that the group members needed several bodyguards with them when they were in public to keep the crowds away.

The group's dance songs generated the most interest. When "I Want You Back" was released in Germany, the song quickly appeared on the music charts. It made it into the top 10 in only three weeks, becoming the fastest newcomer to hit that mark. The song stayed in the top 10 for 8 weeks, the longest stay for a new act in the top 10. *NSYNC proved they were not a one-hit wonder with a popular second release, "Tearin' Up My Heart," which quickly went to number four. "I have hardly ever witnessed newcomers enter the German charts with such incredible, rocket-like speed,"[7] noted Thomas Stein, president of BMG Music Entertainment for the company's German-speaking territories.

A Semi-Anonymous Life

The group's work in Germany was only the beginning. For three months, *NSYNC toured in Europe, Mexico, South Africa, and Asia. While they gained popularity around the world, they were still relatively unknown in the United States.

Their anonymity in the United States was a reality check when they returned home. The boys were stars when they went out in public in Germany, but they were ordinary people in the United States. They realized they would have to continue working if they were to become known in their own country.

The group's success in Europe also gave the members of *NSYNC time to adjust to fame. Popularity did not crush them suddenly but came to them gradually. The group members had a taste of fame but could also retreat into an anonymous life back home.

When *NSYNC finally came back to the United States, it was a shock for them. They were massively popular in Europe, and when they came back home, they were relatively unknown. However, that was soon to change upon the release of their first album in 1998, the same year this photo was taken.

Boy Bands in the United States

While *NSYNC was establishing their popularity outside the United States, a number of all-male singing groups were on the radio in the United States. These boy bands included Boyz II Men, the Backstreet Boys, Hanson, and 98 Degrees. When their world tour ended, *NSYNC found themselves part of a crowded field.

The competition did not discourage the group members, though. They were determined to prove that they had real musical talent. Their music followed the pop format of other boy bands, but Timberlake believed *NSYNC had more to offer. "We have no problem being compared with people—it's something that's going to happen—but I think our voices bring a real R&B feel to pop tunes,"[8] he said.

Reviewers were inclined to agree. *Billboard* writer Chuck Taylor was impressed by the quality of the group's music. He admitted that they were packaged to appeal to young audiences, but he liked what he heard. He described them as "a quintet of freshly scrubbed young men whose music—surprise—is not only infectious but crisply executed and downright ambitious at times."[9] Most critics saw the group as entertaining but nothing more than a pop act with an attractive image, however.

First-Class Pop

Encouraged by the group's success in Europe, *NSYNC's managers and record company began promoting the group in the United States. The album **NSYNC* was introduced in the United States in April 1998 and quickly became popular. It made it to number two on the Billboard 200 list by October of that year.

Even Timberlake was surprised by the group's rapid success. "That was a little overwhelming," he said. "When I found out the album had gone to No. 2, I was jumping up and down. I didn't know what to say."[10]

With the introduction of their music in the United States, the members of the group were now busier than ever. They began traveling around the country, doing interviews and concerts to get their name out in public. One of *NSYNC's first appearances in the United States was at a concert at Walt Disney World. Sweat poured down their faces as the group danced and sang onstage and then introduced themselves to the crowd after the concert.

The band was relatively unknown when it played the

Disney World concert, but the group soon received nationwide attention. In July, the band members were featured on a Disney Channel special that showed them riding on theme park rides, playing at the NFL Experience at Disney's Wide World of Sports, and making music. In late October, they were chosen to be the warm-up act for entertainer Janet Jackson. In addition, the group performed a Disney holiday concert special and appeared in the Walt Disney World Christmas parade.

"With all of these things, everything has just taken off for these guys," said Ron Geslin, who worked for the group's

*NSYNC is shown here performing in Illinois in 1999, shortly after their debut in the United States.

record company. "There's a certain level of music production, a real mentality on their part, that I think is a cut above what some of the similar groups offer. The songs are good, the vocals are fantastic, and the production is first-class pop music."[11]

Touring the United States

Part of *NSYNC's success stemmed from the attention to detail that the group members paid to the production of their songs as well as their live performances. They layered their voices to give their recordings something special, and when they performed onstage, they made sure that their shows were entertaining.

Performing fan favorites such as "Tearin' Up My Heart," "Here We Go," and "God Must Have Spent a Little More Time on You," the group members delivered an engaging and high-energy show. Whether they were shrugging their shoulders in rhythm, doing flips, or simply jumping to the beat, there was always something for their fans to watch as well as listen to.

The group's first U.S. tour was more successful than they had expected. *NSYNC began their tour playing in theaters and then moved onto larger venues such as arenas, amphitheaters, and stadiums. About 1.4 million people, an average of 15,000 per show, saw their act. The group returned to some cities more than once and received an enthusiastic reception every time.

Their shows became more elaborate as the group became more successful. Playing in larger arenas before bigger audiences allowed for more creativity. "The more success, the bigger the toys are to play with, so now it's getting really fun," Timberlake said. "Now we can use props and think more creatively. Our boundaries are becoming bigger and bigger, and we can fantasize and come up with things on a bigger scale."[12]

The group's entertaining efforts brought in crowds and impressed the critics. A concert in Nashville, Tennessee, began with explosive fireworks and screams from the teen girls in the audience. The performance included video clips and showcased the group's musical ability, as well as their ability

The Tour Life

Touring meant *NSYNC got to ride in limousines and be greeted by screaming fans, but life on the road was not easy. The band members were busy traveling, performing, doing interviews, and meeting fans, and they had little time for sleep. "Right after a concert, we jump on the tour bus, still wearing our sweaty clothes, and travel for eight hours until we get to the next city," Joey Fatone told *Seventeen* magazine. "We only get about four hours of sleep a night."[1]

As the group became more popular, *NSYNC fans devised clever ways to meet the group members. In Germany, two girls pretended to faint and then jumped onstage. At an airport, another girl tried to go through the baggage security machine to get to the group. Another time, a girl hid in a hotel room closet, and a shocked Timberlake found her there.

1. Quoted in Jennifer Paris, "*NSYNC," *Seventeen*, July 1999, p. 86.

Fans would follow *NSYNC wherever they went, including the airport. A group of fans are shown here greeting the group while they were promoting an album in 2000.

to entertain. When they sang "Sailing" as the finale, they were suspended 30 feet (9 m) above the crowd on cables.

Keys to a Harley

With his first big paycheck from *NSYNC, Timberlake bought his mom a special Christmas present. When he was young, she had joked that when he was rich and famous he should buy her a Harley Davidson motorcycle. When his check arrived, Timberlake gave his mom a jewelry box with the keys to a Harley inside.

Boy Band Criticism

The group's rapid success was quickly followed by criticism of their abilities. As hard as they worked to set themselves apart, *NSYNC was one of a number of boy bands delivering similar-sounding songs. Some wondered whether the group was more style than substance, and whether it was selling itself on its members' looks and stylish production numbers rather than real talent.

Timberlake and the other group members maintained that the group had much more to offer and that labeling *NSYNC as simply a teen pop act was unfair. They insisted that they were sincere about their music and sincere about their performances. The group wanted to deliver something their fans would enjoy.

Timberlake did not like to think of the group as a boy band or wonder how long it would all last. He simply concentrated on what he was doing and was content to deliver music that the fans enjoyed. As the youngest member of the group, he did not have a great deal of input or creative control over what they delivered, but he believed in what the group was doing. "As far as image, we're just five guys doing the music that we like to do," he said. "We don't pay too much attention to this boy band phenomenon. We just enjoy what we do and being on top and having fun. We consider ourselves a vocal group, because that's what we started off to do. We just want to entertain."[13]

Adoring Fans

*NSYNC provided more music for their fans by releasing a second album in 1998. This album was holiday themed and called *Home for Christmas*. It contained holiday favorites such as "The First Noel" and an a cappella (without accompaniment) version of "O Holy Night," but also original songs such as "Merry Christmas, Happy Holidays." The combination was appealing enough to land the album in the Billboard top 10.

Meanwhile, during this time, *NSYNC received around 1,500 letters a day, and the group's first album sold 12 million copies. At concerts, fans sang along with the songs and screamed for their favorite group members. Not everyone appreciated the group's combination of looks and talent as much as their young fans did, but it could not be denied that the group generated excitement. "*NSYNC are happening in a major way, and even a non-teen male can see why—they can sing, they can dance, they're cute," wrote David Wild in *Rolling Stone*. "That 'N-Syncing feeling is wholesome but not boring."[14]

"Bye, Bye, Bye"

While *NSYNC was proud of the music they were making, they soon learned that there was a business side to the entertainment industry. If they wanted to make money from their hard work, they had to pay attention to that side as well. They had been concentrating so hard on their music, concerts, and promotions that they had not looked carefully at the contract they had signed in order to become part of the music industry.

*NSYNC quickly gathered a fan base when they debuted in the United States. In 1999, the year after they released their first album, they started to win awards. They are shown here at the American Music Awards in 1999.

Group member Lance Bass encouraged the others to look closely at how much their management was being paid. They felt that their manager and record company were taking too large a slice of the profits. The group sought to switch record labels, and the issue went to court with members of *NSYNC claiming that Lou Pearlman, the group's first manager and head of Trans Continental Records, the company *NSYNC was signed to, had taken advantage of their trust.

Celebrity

Timberlake's career kept him busy as he recorded, toured, and promoted *NSYNC. However, he also found time to enjoy fame and spend the money he was earning.

He indulged in a car collection that included three Mercedes vehicles, two Cadillac Escalades, an Audi TT, a Dodge Viper, a BMW, and a Porsche. He also had five motorcycles and three jet skis. In his three-bedroom home in Orlando, he installed a pinball machine.

Timberlake was in his mid-teens when *NSYNC's popularity began to climb, and he took advantage of the perks that came with the group's success. The teen lived the rock star life. He got into clubs, went to parties, and took risks.

Eventually, Timberlake learned that he had to be selective in what he did. He knew there would be repercussions for the wrong choices. "You just have to remember who you are and what's going to mean the most to you down the road," he said. "Are you going to look back and say, yeah, I really had a good time? Is it going to be worth it?"[1]

1. Quoted in Denise Hensley, "Lustin' for Justin," *Cosmopolitan*, November 2001, p. 80.

The release of the group's second album was delayed by the legal wrangling as the dispute led to lawsuits and countersuits. Eventually the group moved to Jive Records, and in 2000, they released the album *No Strings Attached*. A large theme of this album and the resulting tour was puppetry, which stemmed from the group feeling like puppets controlled by Pearlman and their previous record company. In the music video for "Bye, Bye, Bye," the beginning of the video shows the band being controlled on marionette strings that are eventually cut. Additionally, as *NSYNC's popularity increased, so did the amount of merchandise created. This merchandise went beyond the normal T-shirts a fan might buy and included a board game in which the players would try to get backstage at

*NSYNC is shown here with their marionette dolls. These were a popular merchandise item among fans.

an *NSYNC concert, blankets, Barbie dolls, bobbleheads, Beanie Babies, and marionette dolls. The marionettes were especially popular because they tied in directly with the *No Strings Attached* album, music videos, and tour.

The title *No Strings Attached* reflected *NSYNC's independence. They were now free of their first manager and felt more in control of their music. On their second album, both Timberlake and Chasez got writing credits on some of the songs. When he first became part of the group, Timberlake was content to simply do what the group told him to do. As he became more comfortable with his role in the group, he sought more control over the songs they produced.

No Strings Attached continued the group's successful streak. The 2000 release sold 2.4 million albums in its first week, an industry record, and the single "Bye, Bye, Bye" climbed the charts. Fans were eager to see the entertaining group in person and broke Ticketmaster's single-day sales record for their tour when tickets went on sale in March 2000. The successful group made the cover of *Rolling Stone* magazine, an honor that both impressed and perplexed Timberlake. "When I was a kid, I remember seeing Aerosmith on the cover of *Rolling Stone* and thinking, 'Wow, they're rock stars,'" he recalled. "I mean, they're legitimate rock stars. And when *NSYNC got our first *Rolling Stone* cover, something didn't add up for me. We were definitely not rock stars."[15]

*NSYNC's album *No Strings Attached* marked their departure from their record company and also broke industry records. The group is shown here performing at Madison Square Garden in New York City as part of the No Strings Attached Tour.

A Nagging Feeling

Following the group's second album, a nagging feeling started tugging at Timberlake. He had been using his musical talents and following his dream of being a performer for years, long before *NSYNC existed. The group formed in 1995 and immediately began working hard to build their following. By the time their second album was released in 2000, Timberlake started to feel like he was changing and music was changing. He said years later, "I would wake up every morning feeling this more and more of an urge to step out on my own." He continued, "[I want to] try my own hand as a musician, just by myself."[16] In 2002, he shocked fans and the rest of the group when that was exactly what he did.

Chapter Three

Out of Sync

By being involved in the music business through *NSYNC, Timberlake gained a lot of valuable knowledge about the industry. *NSYNC went through legal troubles with their record company and manager very early in their career. They had performed on massive tours and encountered thousands of screaming fans who would do anything they could to just get a glimpse of the band. Additionally, throughout this process, Timberlake learned exactly what he did not want to do with his career. This realization meant the end of *NSYNC and the beginning of his solo projects, which would catapult him into being a legendary force in the music industry.

First Movie Role

Timberlake's first acting job came from the same television channel he had worked for as a youngster, the Disney Channel. In 2000, at age 19, he made his acting debut in the movie *Model Behavior*. The movie is about an ordinary high school girl switching places with her look-alike, who is a model. Timberlake played the model's boyfriend.

Timberlake's role was a small one, which was fine with him. While he wanted to try acting, he readily admitted to the people at Disney that he was not a polished actor. He had done sketch comedy on *MMC* but no serious acting. He had plenty of experience with performing, however, and showed enough promise to get the role.

As he did with his singing and performing, Timberlake took his work as an actor seriously. He was nervous about performing, but that made him try even harder. Although as a member of a popular boy band he had plenty of opportunities to go out at night, he held back while he was making the movie and focused on his career rather than just having a good time with his friends. He was growing up and accepting responsibility for taking his career in another direction. "When we were shooting the movie [in Toronto], he never went out," executive producer Mike Karz said. "All he did was stay at his hotel and go to the set."[17]

The movie was not a blockbuster, but Timberlake did not mind. It was entertaining for its target audience of Disney Channel viewers. Timberlake had wanted to try something new and was happy to have the opportunity to act. "It wasn't Shakespeare," he said. "I'm not worried about what the critics say about my acting, because it's something I like to do for fun."[18]

Relationship with Britney

Timberlake was in the spotlight for another non-musical reason as well. In 1998, he had quietly begun dating pop star Britney Spears. They had worked together on *MMC* and rekindled their friendship when she became the opening act for *NSYNC's tour. Timberlake was quickly taken by Spears, and their friendship blossomed into romance. "I was in love with her from the start," he said in an interview with *GQ* magazine. "I was infatuated with her from the moment I saw her."[19]

Although they dated, they publicly denied being a couple until summer 2000. They were spotted together at clubs in New York City and at the MTV Video Music Awards, and their desire to keep their relationship quiet only made them more sought-after by photographers. The paparazzi tracked the popular pair as they shopped in Miami Beach and walked down Sunset Boulevard in Los Angeles, California.

Justin Timberlake and Britney Spears were frequently photographed together, and many people followed their relationship. They are shown here in matching denim outfits at the American Music Awards.

The Justin Timberlake Foundation

Once he became a successful singer, Timberlake did more than make music. He also established a foundation that helped children include music in their education.

The Justin Timberlake Foundation, formed in 2001, supported music and theater programs in schools. One of the first schools to receive a donation was Timberlake's old school in Memphis, E. E. Jeter Elementary. "School budgets are cut so often, and the first thing that goes is arts and theater programs," Timberlake told Debra Kaufman of the *Hollywood Reporter*. "My foundation benefits these schools that have had budget cuts."[1] Timberlake wanted to give students an opportunity he did not have when he was young. "I wouldn't be where I am today if I hadn't gone outside of school to study music, since I also attended a school with no music program," he said. "Education is important to me, and I want the kids who have the ambition to have the tools to pursue their dreams."[2]

In private, Timberlake made no secret about how he felt about Spears. He enjoyed making grand romantic gestures to show his affection. On Valentine's Day 2000, he surprised her with a special gift. During a show rehearsal, a note was delivered to Spears from Timberlake, and then a five-piece band came in and played Michael Jackson's "The Lady in My Life."

Spears and Timberlake had known each other before either became famous, since their days of singing duets together on *MMC*. They had spent time together as kids and knew both

In 2002, Timberlake partnered with the American Music Conference, which works with a number of celebrities and organizations to help children learn about music.

1. Quoted in Debra Kaufman, "In the Trenches," *Hollywood Reporter - International Edition*, July 24, 2001, p. 6.

2. Quoted in Kaufman, "In the Trenches."

The Justin Timberlake Foundation donated $200,000 to the Memphis Rock 'n' Soul Museum and Memphis Music Foundation in 2008, as shown here.

the fun-loving and serious sides of the other's personality. They both had been performers since they were children and were well aware of the demands of having a music career at such a young age. They had learned about the manipulative side of the music industry and knew how difficult it could be to find trustworthy people.

Spears appreciated the fact that she could be herself with Timberlake and said they were very relaxed when they were together. "When you're comfortable with someone you love, the silence is the best. And that's how me and J. are. When we're in a room together, we don't have to say anything. It's for real,"[20] she said in *Elle* magazine.

For Timberlake, Spears was his refuge when his career became overwhelming. He enjoyed having someone he could be with and talk to, someone who did not think twice about him being a celebrity. Although their busy careers and hectic schedules meant that they were often apart, they were able to set aside time to be with each other. They were successful enough to call some of the shots in their careers and go where they wanted. "We make time," Timberlake said. "We're both at the point in our careers where we're our own bosses, and we're pretty much self-employed and have the finances to do it."[21]

Dirty Pop

Timberlake's financial security was due to the success enjoyed by *NSYNC. The group's tours, merchandise, and albums were all profitable, and in 2001, the group released their fourth CD. Its title, *Celebrity*, reflected the group's status, and in songs like the title track, group members addressed their popularity and fame. When they performed, they were greeted by screaming fans and girls carrying signs with messages for their favorite band members.

Being a celebrity was not all easy. There were safety issues to consider in addition to the heavy workload that came with touring and performing, but the group did not wallow in self-pity about the difficulties of being stars. Instead, they reveled in the success they had been working toward for years. Timberlake and Chasez took the lead on cowriting and coproducing most of the songs on the album. Timberlake contributed the upbeat single "Pop" and used the album as an opportunity to learn more about songwriting. His goal was to learn more about creating music and experiment with different styles. "When we first got into this, obviously I wasn't a songwriter," he said. "But I knew that I wanted to learn it. I didn't let anybody tell me that I couldn't."[22]

On the *Celebrity* album, *NSYNC moved away from a pure pop sound and added some rhythm and blues music to the mix. Several producers were hired to work on the album, which included a contribution from established musician Stevie Wonder, who played harmonica on Timberlake's ballad "Something Like You." Timberlake was awed to work with such talent. "When Stevie came in to record it, that's when I knew I'd made it," Timberlake said. "I almost cried, just realizing that somebody like him is playing on a song I wrote."[23]

In addition to giving *NSYNC the opportunity to work with many successful people in the music industry, *Celebrity* showcased the group's versatility. The individual personalities of the group members emerged, giving the album a personal touch that contributed to its success. The group members were by now seasoned performers and knew what their fans enjoyed.

Celebrity proved the group was not a fluke. The album sold almost 2 million copies in its first week of release and 4.42 million copies in its first year. To Timberlake, the album represented the group's ability to be more than just a boy band. He did not worry about trying to conform to expectations or a certain sound when he wrote songs for the group. He wrote songs that he believed in. "I don't feel that *NSYNC is just a trend," he said. "All we can do is the music that we feel. I think it spoils the creativity when you have to take external things into consideration."[24]

Gone

The group supported the album with a U.S. tour that featured elaborate productions of their songs. The PopOdyssey Tour featured multiple stages and used so much equipment that dozens of trucks were needed to carry it all. The process of setting up the set's stages, staircases, and harnesses that had the group members flying over the crowd was so elaborate that multiple versions of the stage were produced, so the process could begin in one city while they performed in another.

This elaborate tour was followed by another the following spring, although smaller in scale. The group was part of the 2002 Celebrity Tour, performing with acts that included Puff Daddy, Ginuwine, and Smash Mouth. This tour was the group's last, however, as Timberlake and the other group members began to look at taking their careers beyond the boy band.

Timberlake still enjoyed being part of the group, but he also questioned where his career was heading. As popular as the group was, he felt it had limited appeal. He had slowly but surely come to the forefront of the group and felt it was time to see what he could do on his own. He was a fan favorite out of the group's members. He was also a talented musician and performer whose success stemmed from his ability as well as his desire. Name

*NSYNC is shown here on the PopOdyssey Tour. The massive tour required multiple buses to transport the stages, harnesses, and props that they needed for their set design. One of the parts of the show involved them standing on pillars above the stage, which allowed fans in seats farther away to get a better view of the group.

recognition and talent gave Timberlake a strong head start as he struck out on his own.

After the Celebrity Tour, the band felt like they needed some time away to relax and rest. They had been going almost nonstop since 1995, first with trying to get the band started, and then in a span of four years, they released four albums and went on numerous tours. Fans were led to believe that the band was drained from the lifestyle and needed a brief hiatus. Additionally, Timberlake could not ignore the nagging feeling that he wanted to do something else. He said, "[I] felt like the whole thing was too big … It started as a fun snowball fight that was becoming an avalanche. And, also, I was growing out of it. I felt like I cared more about the music than some other people in the group. And I felt like I had other music I wanted to make and that I needed to follow my heart."[25]

In 2002, Timberlake released his solo album, and as each band member tried out new projects, the status of the group became murkier. Chasez stated in 2018 that each member wanted to try something different than what they had been doing for the past seven years. Lance Bass applied to go on a shuttle launch with the Russian Space Agency, Joey Fatone appeared in the movie *My Big Fat Greek Wedding*, and JC Chasez recorded a solo album of his own. The group had enjoyed enormous success, but the members wanted to explore other options for their careers. They did not officially break up, and some members even thought that the hiatus was temporary and Timberlake's solo career was just a brief experiment of working on different music. Fatone said in 2018:

> *We thought we were getting back together … It was, OK, after [Justin] does his thing, blah, blah, blah, we'll get back together and move forward and do what we got to do. And then it was like, nope. The record company wanted to push Justin, I guess, is what it was. He got bigger and bigger, which is honestly great for him and I'm totally happy for him in that sense, but it was more or less weird that there wasn't an explanation to say we're not going to do it, period.*[26]

It took five years for the breakup to be confirmed, and that occurred in Bass's book *Out of Sync*, released in 2007. He wrote, "We're definitely broken up. It's not a hiatus. Justin made it clear that he wouldn't be interested in discussing another album any time soon."[27]

In 2018, the group briefly reunited for a ceremony in California in which they received a star on the Hollywood Walk of Fame. Even at this event, fans were chanting for the group to reunite. As of 2019, that reunion is not in the works except for the brief reunion of four of the members at Coachella that year.

"Cry Me a River"

Timberlake was pursuing his own music career and was soon on his own in other ways as well. His relationship with Spears ran into trouble in 2002. They found it more difficult to find time to be together, and Timberlake suspected Spears was cheating on him, although this was never confirmed. This suspicion was obvious in the lyrics and video for "Cry Me a River" off of Timberlake's first solo album, *Justified*, which was released in late 2002. The lyrics are focused on a cheating partner in a relationship, and the video features a lookalike of Spears. Their relationship ended after nearly four years together.

Timberlake was genuinely hurt when their relationship ended. He could not even say the word "breakup" in an interview, stating that it was too painful to say aloud. He admitted that he cried himself to sleep.

The pair had a public relationship, and their breakup was newsworthy as well. There was much speculation that the two would get back together, but there was also talk of Spears dating others. That hurt Timberlake even more. "I feel like I'm in the middle of a soap opera," he said. "I honestly know what it's like to have a broken heart now."[28]

Timberlake also reflected on the good times he and Spears shared and the good things she had brought to his life. He said he still loved Spears and always would. "I can't sit here and say that she's been a dark part of my life," he said. "She's been a big sunshine in my life. I've learned so many things."[29]

In April 2018, *NSYNC received their star on the Hollywood Walk of Fame.

Trust, Love, and Communication

After breaking up with Britney Spears, Justin Timberlake outlined his rules for making a relationship work. They included love, communication, and trust. Love is the basis for everything, he explained to Michelle Tauber of *People* magazine in 2002. "You start to have a chemistry with someone, and then you fall in love."[1]

Communication was important, he added. "So many times when you date, you don't really communicate," he said. "You think it's okay to not say how you feel because the whole butterflies-in-your-stomach vibe that you keep getting every time you see the person is cute."[2]

Finally, he noted that a relationship will not work without trust. "If you didn't communicate with that person from the very beginning, they can't trust you. If you communicated to that person everything you were feeling and you said exactly how you felt, and you woke up every morning doing what you thought was right and that person did not trust you, then there's nothing you can do at that point and you have to walk away."[3]

1. Michelle Tauber, et al., "Justin Timberlake," *People*, June 24, 2002, p. 58.

2. Quoted in Tauber, et al., "Justin Timberlake."

3. Quoted in Tauber, et al., "Justin Timberlake."

Evaluating a New Career

Timberlake went through a lot in one year—*NSYNC went on their last tour, he and Spears broke up, and he needed to figure out what direction he wanted his career to go in. After focusing so much on *NSYNC's progress and building and maintaining that fan base, he wanted to slow down for a while and also consider what he wanted to do. He said, "I want to enjoy the simple things. I want to take three days off when I want to, not when it's on my calendar. I want to go run in the park with my sweats on because I can. That's where I'm at right now."[30] In addition to all that happened to him personally in 2002, Timberlake started recording music on his own, releasing his first solo album, *Justified*, in November.

Chapter Four

Beginning a Solo Career

The year 2002 was a big one for Timberlake, filled with a lot of major life events. By leaving *NSYNC to try out a solo career, he took a major risk. There was no guarantee that the album or his career would be successful and go the way he wanted it to, especially when he was breaking away from a massively popular group and creating his own sound. However, he used the knowledge gained from his years with *NSYNC, as well as his desire to perform and develop his own style, and ended up proving that there was more to him than being a member of *NSYNC.

A New, Diverse Sound

On *Justified*, Timberlake wanted to be known for more complex music than the pop songs *NSYNC had produced. While *NSYNC's music had been enjoyable to teens and preteens, it was not something many other artists respected. To develop a richer and more personal sound, Timberlake added elements of hip-hop, funk, and rhythm and blues styles to his music.

For Timberlake, this was a natural expression of his varied musical interests. He explained that he had eclectic tastes, stemming in part from his roots. Some listeners might have been surprised by his new sound, but to him it was simply an outgrowth of who he was and the musician he was becoming. "In a group, people don't get to see everybody's individual personalities," he said. "They just see the unit. But now they see there is this side of me and it's surprising. But I grew up in Memphis where blues was invented."[31]

Justin Timberlake is shown here performing in 2003 with Pharrell Williams. Pharrell helped create the unique and appealing sound on *Justified*.

"Yoshimi Battles the Pink Robots"

Timberlake showed that he was not afraid to do something unusual when he jammed with the rock group the Flaming Lips in 2003. While in England, he met the group in the hallway at the British television network BBC. He mentioned that he had the group's records, and singer Wayne Coyne asked if Timberlake would like to play with them.

Timberlake agreed to join the band for "Yoshimi Battles the Pink Robots," and he played bass on the song for the British television show *Top of the Pops*. The group wore costumes onstage, so Timberlake put on a dolphin suit. In the final minute, he took off the head of the disguise, to the surprise and delight of the audience.

Timberlake knew better than to try to create these new sounds on his own. With *NSYNC, he had worked with a number of record producers and knew that each brought their own strengths into the studio. For his solo debut, he tapped into his contacts in the music industry. He got help from producers such as Timbaland, Chad Hugo, and Pharrell Williams. These producers helped Timberlake create the unique, appealing, and danceable sound that was his goal.

It took only six weeks to write and record *Justified*. Throughout that time, Timberlake was both directing the album's sound and learning from the people with whom he was working. He appreciated the feedback the producers gave him. "To make an album, it takes both those personalities," he said. "Somebody who's dictating what they definitely want and somebody to be the coach, who can sit on the sidelines and say, 'Yeah, I think that's it.'"[32]

Timberlake is shown here with members of the Flaming Lips.

Autobiographical Songs

A number of the songs on *Justified* reflected Timberlake's independence, both as a musical artist and in his personal life. He was on his own after seven years as part of a popular group. In addition, at the time he was recording the album he was still stinging from his breakup with Spears.

The songs on the album reflected Timberlake's perspective on life at the time. He was anxious about being on his own and suffering from a broken heart. Writing songs for the album became therapeutic as he dealt with many changes. About half the songs on the album were autobiographical, he said, and the other half a fantasy.

The personal nature of the songs on *Justified* showed how much he believed in his new musical venture. Timberlake realized that he could be heavily criticized for his music. However, he needed to try something new if he was to grow as a musician. "If I feel it in my gut, I just leap," he said. "That's my philosophy with everything. If you fall down, you figure it out for the next time."[33]

Controversy Surrounding a Hit

Timberlake's gut feeling about his career move was correct. When his solo debut album was released in November 2002, it was a resounding success. Critics loved it, and it eventually sold more than 4 million copies.

When he listened to the music he and the others had created on *Justified*, Timberlake realized he had achieved exactly what he had set out to do. He had developed a distinct sound for himself and had proven himself as an artist in his own right. He said the music on *Justified* was much better than anything *NSYNC had ever done, and he even gained admiration from Lou Pearlman, who had formed *NSYNC.

The album was the highlight of Timberlake's year, and he was proud of his accomplishment. "I love to be in the studio writing music, and this album is all me," he said. "I am happy with it."[34]

Timberlake's first solo album was not without controversy. The song "Cry Me a River" was said to be about his breakup with Spears, and it looked as if Timberlake was getting back at Spears with the video and song. It implied that Spears cheated on him and that he was the one who was wronged and hurt by their breakup. Fans and the media went crazy with speculation after the song and music video were released.

Timberlake downplayed the controversy of the video, saying that it actually made him look like the one who had done something wrong. The video showed him retaliating by being with another woman and making sure the character who was supposedly Spears knew about it. "What is all the fuss about?" he said. "If anybody is the bad guy in the video, it's me."[35]

When questioned about Spears, Timberlake said he had loved Spears from the moment they met and he had no bad feelings toward her. They still spoke, he said, and maintained a civil, friendly relationship.

Inventing a New Image

The controversy over the "Cry Me a River" video actually helped Timberlake's evolving image. With *NSYNC, he had been a clean-cut member of a group that focused on a core audience of young teens. The group had been wholesome and safe, and as a solo artist, Timberlake was ready to be more daring.

With *Justified*, Timberlake showed an edgier side, not only with his music but with his personality as well. He was still sensitive, as evidenced by the pain he felt over his breakup with Spears, but the way he dealt with his pain in the video suggested a darker side.

Timberlake had to invent a new image as a performer as well. When he toured and made television appearances to promote his new album, he was onstage without the other four singers he had been used to performing with for seven years. He had been in the spotlight in the past, but not for the entire show. Now the success or failure of a performance was all on his shoulders.

Timberlake made his first solo appearance on television on the MTV Video Music Awards (VMAs) in August 2002. Emerging out of a giant boom box, he sang "Like I Love You" and performed dance moves reminiscent of Michael Jackson, a performer he had admired for years. Some people criticized his performance because he dressed so much like Jackson, with gloves and a cocked hat, but Timberlake was making a statement. Like Jackson, who left the Jackson 5 to break out on his own, Timberlake was leaving the group behind and was coming out as a solo act. It was the beginning of a new era.

Timberlake toured the following year to promote his new album, heading to Europe in 2003 for his first solo concerts. He was anxious about performing alone, but once the audience began responding to his music, the performance went fine.

As he had with the production of his album, Timberlake exerted a great deal of control over his solo tour, and he had a clear vision of what he wanted it to be like.

Timberlake performed the controversial hit “Cry Me a River” at the 2002 Billboard Music Awards. He performed most of the song sitting down because he had broken his foot.

YAMAHA
YAMAHA
KORG
KORG

In 2002, Timberlake performed songs from his first solo album at the MTV Video Music Awards.

He used medleys to keep the music flowing continuously and included heavy doses of dancing. “I hate going to a show and feeling like it’s a recital,” he said. “I’d rather it feel continuous, like a club. You go to a club and the DJ doesn’t stop, he just spins from one song to the next.”[36]

Timberlake’s touring schedule was demanding, and it was not easy being out of the United States. Not every show went well. He did a summer concert in Toronto, Canada, in 2003

that was met with a horrible reception. The benefit concert included the Rolling Stones, AC/DC, the Guess Who, and Rush, and Timberlake wondered if the fans at the concert who were there to see the hard rock acts would appreciate his music. He quickly found that they did not. He did three songs before being pelted with water bottles thrown by the crowd.

The show in Toronto, however, was the exception to the rule. Most crowds adored him. Timberlake was happy to be admired for what he could do, not just because he was a star. "It's a liberating thing to walk onstage and see people your age and up," he said. "And they're not screaming just because you're standing there, they're screaming because you did something to impress them. They don't put your poster on their wall—they just like your record."[37]

Fame

That summer, he toured in the United States as well. Joining him was former Mouseketeer Christina Aguilera, whose voice he admired and who had also recently been at the top of the pop music charts. They did not perform together in the concert, but each took their turn with solo performances. Timberlake's show was impressive; he brought a 14-piece band with him on the road, climbed on a crane during the performance, and used video images to entertain the crowd.

The tour gave him something else he did not often have: privacy. When he did not have to be onstage he could go to his dressing room and prepare for the performance, alone. "I crave alone time," he said. He added,

I think sometimes you get these people who become obsessed with the four-letter word fame. To me, it doesn't exist. There's

Christina Aguilera and Justin Timberlake formerly starred on *MMC* together and rejoined later for a joint tour to promote their new albums. The pair did not perform any songs together, but each performed a full set of songs with elaborate stage setups.

nothing that says that any of us entertainers are a pinky nail in length more important than the guy who builds the streets in New York City. I mean, he's doing a lot more than I am for society.[38]

Timberlake did not become reclusive, however. He needed some time to himself but remained sociable. After the show was over for the night, he did not stop performing. He would often do an after-show performance at a small club. He and his band would make music without scenery, props, or choreographed dances. This helped him grow musically and gain more credibility as a performer and musician.

In addition to bringing him respect, *Justified* brought Timberlake awards. In 2003, he won an award at the VMAs for Best Dance Video for "Rock Your Body." He also won two Grammy Awards for the album. His music brought him compliments from his peers in the music industry. When he was applauded by rap artists 50 Cent and Eminem after he received the award for Best Male Video at the VMAs, he saw it as an accomplishment. He was surprised and relieved that they respected him and his music.

"That Guy from the Boy Band"

Leaving *NSYNC and branching out on his own was a huge risk for Timberlake. It was a risk that ended up paying off. He was making the music he wanted to make and making it how he wanted to make it. He had created his own sound and completely broken away from the bubblegum pop *NSYNC was producing. "The whole year was weird for me," he said. "Before that, I was just a boy in a group. There was a lot of naiveté involved, and we didn't really understand the weight of the phenomenon."[39]

Eventually, Timberlake started to feel like people were actually listening to his music and enjoying it. Additionally, he was gaining new fans that might not have enjoyed *NSYNC's music when he was still with the group. Timberlake said, "I didn't want to be that 'guy from the boy band'... I didn't want to be that guy who is just, like, famous for being famous. I didn't want to be the guy who dates girls in the tabloids. That's why the album was such a big deal for me. I had to fight harder for my respect, my credibility."[40]

Timberlake had proven to himself and others that he could branch off from *NSYNC and be known for his own talents rather than as that member of a boy band. Next, he had to prove that he would have more than just one hit album.

Chapter Five

Branching Out Beyond Music

Timberlake was using his talents to create the music he wanted to, but he did not want to stick with just the music industry any longer. He had proven himself as a musician, but he wanted to try new things. Without *NSYNC's rigorous touring and recording schedule, he was able to think about other projects he wanted to take on, and acting was a natural choice.

Saturday Night Live

There was no shortage of work for Timberlake in the entertainment industry. He rekindled his television career with an appearance on *Saturday Night Live* (*SNL*) in 2003. A perfectionist at whatever he did, he prepared thoroughly for his time onstage. Although he was the show's guest host, he did not rely on the show's regulars to carry his performance. He wanted to contribute and have the audience enjoy his appearance.

Timberlake was comfortable in front of a live audience and was used to sketch comedy from his days on *MMC*. He surprised many viewers as well as those in the audience with his adept turn at humor. His acting, delivery, and timing were impressive as he confidently dressed like entertainer Jessica Simpson and impersonated actor Ashton Kutcher.

Additionally, he performed "Cry Me a River," "Rock Your Body," and "Señorita."

Cameron Diaz

As Timberlake took some time away from music, he deepened his relationship with a new girlfriend. He began dating actress Cameron Diaz in 2003, after they met at the Nickelodeon Kids' Choice Awards. Diaz was a Los Angeles native, a model, and an actress who had appeared in movies such as *The Mask*, *There's*

Cameron Diaz and Justin Timberlake are shown here at a Los Angeles Lakers basketball game.

Something About Mary, and *Charlie's Angels*. She was also the voice of Princess Fiona in the animated film *Shrek*.

Diaz was older than Timberlake, 31 to his 22, but despite their nine-year age difference, the pair had much in common. Both were interested in the outdoors and sports. They vacationed in Hawaii, where they surfed and enjoyed relaxing on the beach.

Their relationship did not go unnoticed by the press. They had to deal with interest from the tabloid press whenever they were together, and their vacation was interrupted by the many photographers looking to get a picture of the couple. By now, however, Timberlake was a veteran at dealing with fame. He convinced photographers to keep a certain distance away from him and Diaz. He had just left a celebrity relationship that had been well chronicled by the press and did what he could to control the intrusion this time.

Super Bowl 2004

In February 2004, Timberlake appeared with Janet Jackson for the Super Bowl halftime show. The show was filled with other stars, including Kid Rock, P. Diddy (formerly known as Puff Daddy), and Nelly, and the pair was looking for something to set their duet apart. To make it memorable, they planned to do a "reveal" at the end of their number by pulling off a piece of her wardrobe.

At first, they considered using a long skirt, but Jackson found the skirt too difficult to dance in. They then decided to rig her bodice—the top of her outfit—so red fabric would be revealed when Timberlake pulled it downward. Their plan for a big reveal worked too well. At the end of the number, Timberlake grabbed Jackson's bodice and ripped downward. It was supposed to reveal the red fabric, but it exposed Jackson's breast on live TV.

The resulting uproar over the incident led to cries of indecency and later resulted in a fine for the network. There were questions about whether or not the incident was planned, and Timberlake apologized for the indecent scene on the Grammy Awards show the next week. After he won the award for male pop vocal for "Cry Me a River," he said, "I know it's been a rough week on everybody … What occurred was unintentional, completely regrettable, and I apologize if you guys were offended."[41]

Some wondered if Timberlake got off too easily, while Jackson bore the brunt of the negative publicity. There was criticism for

Super Bowl Controversy

In 2004, Janet Jackson was the center of controversy following the 2004 Super Bowl performance with Timberlake. During the show, Timberlake ripped the front of her costume, exposing her breast on live TV. She immediately covered herself with a look of shock on her face. However, in the end, Jackson took the blame and the heaviest hit for the incident. In a taped apology, Jackson accepted responsibility for her shirt ripping. Meanwhile, Jackson was barred from attending both the Grammy Awards and MTV Video Music Awards while Timberlake was able to attend without a problem. Additionally, Jackson has not had a single song reach the top 10 since the 2004 Super Bowl. In 2015, Jackson released her first album since 2008 and performed a 56-date State of the World Tour in 2017. The album was appropriately titled *Unbreakable*, and it was widely praised. It took Jackson years to get her career back, while Timberlake released three acclaimed albums between the 2004 Super Bowl and 2015.

In 2018, Timberlake released his fourth solo album, *Man of the Woods*, and performed at the Super Bowl. It was with this Super Bowl performance that he started receiving backlash for the 2004 Super Bowl. When it was announced that he would be the performer at the 2018 Super Bowl, #JusticeForJanet spread across him not supporting her more strongly. Timberlake admitted that Jackson was the one who carried most of the burden in the uproar that followed. The incident certainly did not hurt his popularity. He continued to try new projects in his time away from the studio and tour, and he remained a singer who was in demand.

The 2004 Super Bowl halftime show generated a lot of controversy for both Timberlake and Jackson. The pair are shown here performing at the Super Bowl before Jackson's costume was ripped.

Twitter, with users criticizing the fact that Timberlake was asked to perform again at the Super Bowl while Jackson had not performed at the event since 2004. Twitter users even rebranded the day of the Super Bowl in 2018 as #JanetJacksonAppreciationDay. Throughout the day, users posted clips of some of her most memorable performances and achievements to show support for her, and it was trending more on Twitter than the Super Bowl itself on the day of the Super Bowl.

Helping Other Artists

Timberlake tried to stay out of the public eye after the Super Bowl, but he did not abandon music completely. Always interested in new musical styles, he showed that he could appeal to fans of many different types of music by appearing on Snoop Dogg's hit song "Signs." He also showed up on the album *Monkey Business* by the Black Eyed Peas, a group he had also worked with on their *Elephunk* CD.

Timberlake showed that he did not have to always be the star of the show. He was content to make music and be in the background as he collaborated with other artists. His time with *NSYNC had taught him the value of working as part

Justin Timberlake did not only work on his own music; he also made guest appearances on other artists' music. He is shown here performing at a Black Eyed Peas concert.

of a group. Working alongside a rap artist or hip-hop group helped Timberlake's reputation as well and cast him as a musician who appealed to a broad audience.

Making Edison

Timberlake did not yet have the energy to return to the recording studio or go on tour, but he did not abandon his career. He went in a new direction, away from music and toward movies with an appearance in the movie *Edison*. He played an investigative journalist in the thriller starring Morgan Freeman and Kevin Spacey.

The movie was filmed in Vancouver, Canada, during the summer of 2004, and the experience allowed him to continue to find enjoyment in acting the way he did while hosting *SNL*. "*SNL* was like a playground," he said. "And the reason I got into film is because I needed something inspiring, but more intimate, that I didn't have to do in front of 180,000 people every night."[42]

Making *Edison* was much more involved than sketch comedy, however. The full-length film meant going on location to make the movie and spending days on the set. In addition to learning his lines and working on his acting, he also had to deal with fans who camped out on the street outside his rented home. He dealt with them by bringing along his own security staff while on location.

Timberlake had a large supporting role in the movie and was billed third following the film's two stars. His second foray into acting did not receive a great deal of attention, however, as the film received mediocre reviews and went straight to video.

Throat Surgery and Rest

This time spent acting and working on side projects allowed Timberlake to get the rest he needed. In 2005, he underwent surgery to remove throat nodules. Throat nodules are small growths on the vocal cords, and these could greatly affect his career. As a result of the surgery, he had to rest his voice

Clothing Line

When Timberlake took a break from recording in 2005, he dabbled in fashion. He had a well-known name and a solid image that could be used effectively to market things besides music. With his friend Trace Ayala, he started the William Rast clothing line. It was named after Justin's grandfather, William, and Ayala's grandfather, whose last name was Rast.

Timberlake and Trace Ayala are shown here at an event for the William Rast clothing line.

as much as he could for three months following the surgery. This time spent recovering gave Timberlake the ability to relax and live life at a more regular pace. Timberlake said, “That was amazing for me … Just the little things, like sitting home on the weekend or making a Sunday tee time.”[43] Following his recovery, he went back into the studio to work on the long-awaited follow-up to *Justified*.

Chapter Six

New Directions

Timberlake came back from his much-needed resting time after throat surgery ready to record new music. However, he did not want to re-create the same album he did before. He wanted to try something new and take chances. Once again, these risks paid off and proved that Timberlake was a force who would have staying power in the music industry. Following his second solo album, *FutureSex/LoveSounds*, Timberlake's solo career really took off, and he released the two-part album *The 20/20 Experience*, which also featured respected rap artist JAY-Z. During this time, Timberlake met the love of his life, actress Jessica Biel, who he would marry and later have a son with.

Experimenting with Music

As Timberlake prepared to make his new album, he felt he could create something that was better than the music he heard being played on the radio. He wanted to bring a new sound to the airwaves. "I knew that I needed something new," he said. "I wanted to take more of a chance—experiment."[44]

He began recording the new album in December 2005, spending a few weeks in the studio and then taking a few weeks off. He was by now very familiar with all aspects of creating music, from writing songs to the technology that went into production, and was heavily involved in the entire process. The popular record producer and rapper Timbaland had helped out on Timberlake's previous album with tracks such as "Cry Me a River" and also contributed to the music and vocals on Timberlake's new CD. He was amazed by how everyone in the studio worked together and contributed. "Everybody's creativity was at a peak, and everybody was just throwing ideas into the pot,"[45] he said.

Timberlake came up with the songs' lyrics, verses, bridges, and choruses while they were in the studio. His ability to put a song together without writing down the words impressed those he worked with. "Everybody knows he's talented, but this dude wrote that whole album without touching a pen or paper," said producer Nate "Danja" Hills. "I've heard stories about JAY-Z or Biggie doing that, but I've never heard of a singer doing that. I think it's some sort of superpower."[46]

Timberlake enjoyed the creative process, but although he had been enormously successful with his previous album, he was not confident about how this one would be received. When he made *Justified*, he had little to lose and everything to gain from being creative and innovative as he worked to build a reputation. Now, people expected more from him, and he worried about living up to those expectations. He sometimes had nightmares about whether his music would be accepted.

However, Timberlake need not have worried. *FutureSex/LoveSounds* was considered by many to be edgy, innovative, and danceable, and as good, or better, than its predecessor. Timberlake had made a record that could appeal to fans of many styles of music. Innovative hits such as "SexyBack," "My Love," and "What Goes Around…/…Comes Around" received a great deal of radio airplay. The album was also popular in nightclubs, as its songs were made for dancing. Timberlake was reaching out to varied audiences with his album, from hip-hop fans to listeners who liked dance music. He was rewarded for his efforts with two Grammys for *FutureSex/LoveSounds*. He and Timbaland won for Best Dance Recording for "SexyBack" and Best Rap/Sung Collaboration for "My Love," which featured rapper T.I.

Evolving the Onstage Image

Along with the new sound, Timberlake's image continued to evolve onstage as well. *Justified* had earned him respect and had proved that he had the talent to become a solo artist. With his second solo effort, he took another step. With shows at clubs such as the House of Blues, he moved even further away from his boy band past and began entrenching himself in the music industry as an artist with staying power. In his club concerts, Timberlake impressed the audience by concentrating on music rather than dancing or flashy lights. He led a band, played keyboard and guitar, and sang vocals. He also showed that he had wide appeal by including an appearance by the hip-hop group Three 6 Mafia and producer and singer Timbaland in his show.

In addition to playing small clubs, Timberlake also performed before much larger audiences as he toured to promote his new album. Appearing at Madison Square Garden in 2007 before a sold-out audience, he delivered a performance that highlighted his musical talent as well as his ability as a performer. He provided funky beats, played keyboards, and even did some comedy with *Saturday Night Live*'s Andy Samberg. He danced with elaborate choreography and used video screens, lighting effects, and a central stage to add interest to his performance. His music was "as if the funk of the future had finally arrived," wrote Gavin Edwards of *Rolling Stone*. "Timberlake commanded the crowd's attention just by striding around the stage that was unquestionably his."[47]

Jessica Biel

In 2006, Timberlake and Diaz ended their relationship. After three years together, they publicly announced that they were no longer a couple. There was a lot of speculation about why they broke up, but they had not been very open about their relationship when they were together and were just as discreet when they broke up. They released a statement that said that although it had been their practice not to comment on their relationship, they felt compelled to do so because of speculation and inaccurate stories.

After splitting with Diaz, he was linked to actress Jessica Biel. In 2007, Biel and Timberlake admitted that they were in a relationship. They were frequently photographed together at events such as the Met Gala and on their way to Broadway shows, such as *Hamilton* creator Lin-Manuel Miranda's *In the Heights*. Biel and Timberlake were together for four years before they broke up in early 2011. However, Timberlake realized that he did not enjoy being single—particularly, he did not enjoy being without Biel in his life. The couple got back together in the summer of 2011, and in January 2012, they were engaged to be married. Biel and Timberlake were married in October 2012 after being engaged for 10 months. Three years later, in 2015, Biel gave birth to their first child, Silas Randall. As of 2019, the couple has been together nearly 11 years and are supportive of each other's careers. Timberlake supports Biel at award shows for her acting career, and she makes appearances at his concerts and in his music videos, such as the one for "Man of the Woods" off of the 2018 album of the same name. They also frequently share photos of moments from their relationship on their social media accounts, and Timberlake has written songs about Biel. For example, "Montana" off of the *Man of the Woods* album has special meaning because Timberlake proposed to Biel in Montana. The song "Mirrors" off of *The 20/20 Experience* is also about Biel and their relationship.

Acting Career

Despite the disappointing outcome of *Edison*, Timberlake fed his interest in acting with a number of supporting roles. "Justin could have had a starring role," said director Craig Brewer, who directed Timberlake in the 2006 film *Black Snake Moan*. "But he's aware that audiences are cynical about music stars crossing over into acting."[48]

In 2007, Justin Timberlake and Jessica Biel started dating. They were married in 2012. They are shown here in 2018 at the Emmy Awards.

In *Black Snake Moan*, Timberlake played a member of the National Guard who has anxiety. The film starred Samuel L. Jackson and Christina Ricci, and Brewer felt Timberlake could bring the depth needed for his smaller role as a troubled young man. "When I approached him for it I said, 'It's a vulnerable role, and I really want you to tap into something.' He understood that,"[49] said Brewer.

Timberlake's next film fared better, as he again expanded his acting range and moved even further away from the good-boy pop star image that had made him a star. In *Alpha Dog*, he played Frankie Ballenbacher, a tough guy who assists with a kidnapping. The movie was based on the true story of the kidnapping and murder of Nick Markowitz. Timberlake's reputation as a singer made one of his costars unsure of him as an actor, but once filming started, he earned her respect. "I really wasn't sure about him because he's a singer," said Amanda Seyfried, who acted with him in *Alpha Dog*. "But he blows me away."[50]

In 2010, Timberlake started in another true story, *The Social Network*, which was about the founding of Facebook. Timberlake played Sean Parker, who was a cofounding president of Facebook.

Hindsight

In 2018, Timberlake became an author when he released *Hindsight: & All the Things I Can't See in Front of Me*. The book featured many photos from throughout Timberlake's career and also included personal details, such as his thoughts on being a father and husband. He also included his thoughts on his rise to fame, his past with *NSYNC, and his friendship with Jimmy Fallon. Along with the positive points of his career, Timberlake also evaluated his mistakes and missteps, allowing fans a glimpse into his personal life and thought process.

The movie received positive reviews, as did Timberlake's performance as Parker. *Rolling Stone* wrote in its review of the movie, "Timberlake is phenomenal, a revelation, even. You expect him to nail Sean's charming hustle, and he does … It's a role to die for, and Timberlake the mesmerizer just crushes it."[51]

In 2016, Timberlake provided a voice for the character of Branch in the animated movie *Trolls*. He also provided the infectious hit song "Can't Stop the Feeling!" for the film. The song is an upbeat, fun song that Timberlake continues to perform on tour. Timberlake reprised his role of Branch for the 2020 *Trolls* sequel, *Trolls World Tour*.

Timberlake is shown here at a *Trolls* movie premiere, with (from left) Christopher Mintz-Plasse, Kunal Nayyar, Anna Kendrick, James Corden, Zooey Deschanel, and Icona Pop.

The 20/20 Experience

There were seven years in between the release of *FutureSex/ LoveSounds* and the two-part album *The 20/20 Experience*. During this time, Timberlake had filled his career with acting roles and found plenty of inspiration for future music, including his wife, Jessica Biel. After *FutureSex/LoveSounds*, Timberlake did not have to prove what he could do anymore. Additionally, with more than 11 years since the last *NSYNC album, he did not have to try to break away from that image any further. The result was a two-part album that found Timberlake in a more relaxed point of his life, which was evident in the style of music throughout the albums. Both parts of *The 20/20 Experience* feature ambitious, long songs that had hints of R&B, soul, and pop all blended together for a unique sound. Timbaland joined Timberlake again on this album by coproducing every song, and JAY-Z was featured on fan favorite hits such as "Suit & Tie." The album featured infectious, percussive songs such as "Don't Hold the Wall" and "Let the Groove Get In," which were listed in album reviews as some of the best songs on the record.

In the fall of 2013, the second part of *The 20/20 Experience* was released and featured hits such as "TKO," "Drink You Away," and "Take Back the Night." Critics praised Timberlake for his remarkable, rare album. *Rolling Stone* stated, "Other artists roar like lions and bang like gorillas to get our attention. Having spent years proving himself a full-spectrum superstar in Hollywood and on *Saturday Night Live*, JT glided back to music with a 70-minute-plus LP of adventurous, stretched-out neosoul vamps."[52] Other critics, however, viewed the second part of the album as filler songs or leftovers that did not make it onto the first album.

One thing that was incorporated into both parts of the album was the 25-piece band the Tennessee Kids. The Tennessee Kids are Timberlake's band, and he does not treat them as merely his backing music. They are an important part of his albums and his concerts, and he introduces them and gives them their time to shine. Timberlake's time with *NSYNC gave him valuable knowledge about the industry and how to be part of an ensemble, and this knowledge is evident in how he treats his band.

The Tennessee Kids are an important part of Timberlake's albums and live shows. The Tennessee Kids and Timberlake are shown here performing during the 20/20 Experience World Tour.

He respects his band, which was obvious in the Netflix concert documentary of the 20/20 Experience Tour. The concert special did not have just Timberlake's name in the title: it also had the Tennessee Kids.

Album Misstep

Justin Timberlake tends to have many years in between album releases. It allows him to enjoy time with his family, pursue side projects, and focus on writing new music in the way that he wants to. Timberlake's next album was no exception. *Man of the Woods* was released in early 2018, right before Timberlake's Super Bowl halftime show. The album contains many personal songs, such as "Young Man," which is written about his son, and "Montana," which is the state that Timberlake and Biel got engaged in. However, even though this album had personal songs, it was categorized as a weaker album of Timberlake's. While fans loved it, critics stated the songs were shallow and the overall album was a misstep for Timberlake.

The Man of the Woods Tour involved a massive stage that stretched from one end of an arena to another. During one song in the concert, Timberlake performed in front of what was supposed to be a campfire.

The problems surrounding this album continued to grow when Timberlake had to cancel some tour dates on the Man of the Woods Tour. In some places, even the rescheduled dates were canceled, and eventually the entire tour was canceled and rescheduled. This was due to additional problems with Timberlake's vocal cords. His vocal cords were severely bruised, and he was directed to rest his voice as much as possible. When he did make it back onto the road to finish the tour, he made it worth the fans' wait. The Man of the Woods Tour had a massive stage design that required multiple buses. The design of the stage allowed fans in multiple parts of the arenas to have a good view. The stage expanded from one end of the floor in an arena to the other end of the floor and included many screens that would show videos at certain times and lighted trees highlighting certain parts of the stage. Additionally, Timberlake sang songs from his entire solo career, allowing fans to hear favorites such as "My Love," "SexyBack," and "Cry Me a River."

The Future

Justin Timberlake is a rare pop star. He developed his musical talents as a child and continued to make a career out of them—even when many believed at some point it would all end for him. While he became well known as a result of his role as a fan favorite member of *NSYNC, he proved that this role was not the only one he would be known for. He also proved that he had immense talent and could make each album and each song sound completely different from anything that came before. This rare ability was recognized in May 2019 when it was announced that Timberlake would receive the Contemporary Icon award at the Songwriters Hall of Fame. The award is given to "a songwriter-artist who has attained an iconic status in pop culture."[53] Songwriters Hall of Fame chairman Nile Rodgers said Timberlake has "turned pop music into great art and made three or four of the most influential albums of the last 15 years … He knows the secret is extraordinary songs. He and Timbaland have defined an era."[54]

Also in May 2019, Timberlake received an honorary doctorate degree from the Berklee College of Music for his contributions to music. Whether it is acting or creating completely unique and extraordinary music, the future looks bright for Justin Timberlake as he continues to be a widely respected and admired musician.

Notes

Introduction: *Justified*

1. Brittany Spanos, "Justin Timberlake's 'FutureSex/LoveSounds': 10 Things You Didn't Know," *Rolling Stone*, September 8, 2016. www.rollingstone.com/music/music-news/justin-timberlakes-futuresex-lovesounds-10-things-you-didnt-know-121060/.

Chapter One: Tennessee Kid

2. Quoted in Austin Scaggs, "Justin Timberlake Revs Up His Sex Machine," *Rolling Stone*, September 21, 2006, p. 50.

3. Quoted in Jeremy Helligar, et al., "Boy Power," *People*, February 8, 1999, p. 93.

4. Quoted in Anthony Breznican, "Timberlake Turns Away from Spotlight," *USA Today*, May 1, 2007, p. 01d.

Chapter Two: Tearin' Up Fans' Hearts

5. Quoted in Taylor Weatherby, "*NSYNC Reflects on Making U.S. Debut & Competing With Backstreet Boys as Self-Titled Album Turns 20: 'It Was Us Against the World,'" *Billboard*, March 24, 2018. www.billboard.com/articles/columns/pop/8258181/nsync-debut-album-us-20th-anniversary-oral-history.

6. Quoted in Chuck Taylor, "Following Its Soulful Instincts, RCS's 'NSync Set to Break Away from Boy-Group Brigade," *Billboard*, April 18, 1998, p. 72.

7. Quoted in Wolfgang Spahr, "Ariola Act Is *NSYNC with German Fans," *Billboard*, June 21, 1997, p. 47.

8. Quoted in Taylor, "Following Its Soulful Instincts, RCS's 'NSync Set to Break Away from Boy-Group Brigade."

9. Taylor, "Following Its Soulful Instincts, RCS's 'NSync Set to Break Away from Boy-Group Brigade."

10. Quoted in Chuck Taylor, "*NSYNC Spends Its 'Time' Evolving Into More Than Just a Teen Pop Sensation," *Billboard*, November 7, 1999, p. 104.

11. Quoted in Taylor, "*NSYNC Spends Its 'Time' Evolving Into More Than Just a Teen Pop Sensation."
12. Quoted in Taylor, "*NSYNC Spends Its 'Time' Evolving Into More Than Just a Teen Pop Sensation."
13. Quoted in Taylor, "*NSYNC Spends Its 'Time' Evolving Into More Than Just a Teen Pop Sensation."
14. David Wild, "NSync," *Rolling Stone*, November 12, 1998, p. 59.
15. Quoted in Jenny Eliscu, "Justin Grows Up," *Rolling Stone*, May 18, 2006, p. 210.
16. Quoted in Anita Bennett, "Justin Timberlake: Leaving 'N Sync Was 'One of the Best/Worst Things That I Have Ever Done,'" *E! News*, May 12, 2014. www.eonline.com/news/541182/justin-timberlake-leaving-n-sync-was-one-of-the-best-worst-things-that-i-have-ever-done.

Chapter Three: Out of Sync

17. Quoted in Dave Karger, "And Justin for All," *Entertainment Weekly*, March 10, 2000, p. 57.
18. Quoted in Jason Lynch, "Talking with…Justin Timberlake," *People*, March 13, 2000, p. 32.
19. Quoted in ABC News, "Justin on Britney: 'In Love From the Start.'" www.abcnews.go.com/print?id=2217905.
20. Quoted in Dan Jewel, "Pop's Puppy Lovers," *People*, November 27, 2000, p. 85.
21. Quoted in Denise Hensley, "Lustin' for Justin," *Cosmopolitan*, November 2001, p. 80.
22. Quoted in Rebecca Wallwork, "Justin Timberlake," *Interview*, February 2003, p. 48.
23. Quoted in Denise Hensley, "Lustin' for Justin."
24. Quoted in Denise Hensley, "Lustin' for Justin."
25. Quoted in Adam Silvers, "Justin Timberlake Reveals Real Reason He Left *NSYNC," Elite Daily, February 8, 2017. www.elitedaily.com/entertainment/celebrity/justin-timberlake-reason-leave-nsync/1784243.

26. Quoted in Leigh Blickley, "A History of *NSYNC's Breakup, According to Bandmates Not Named Justin Timberlake," *Huffington Post*, updated February 14, 2019. www.huffpost.com/entry/nsync-interview-walk-of-fame_n_5ade1b2be4b0df502a4e64d0.

27. Quoted in Blickley, "A History of *NSYNC's Breakup, According to Bandmates Not Named Justin Timberlake."

28. Quoted in Michelle Tauber, et al., "Justin Timberlake," *People*, June 24, 2002, p. 58.

29. Quoted in Tauber, et al., "Justin Timberlake."

30. Quoted in Tauber, et al., "Justin Timberlake."

Chapter Four: Beginning a Solo Career

31. Quoted in "Justin Timberlake," *Newsweek*, November 11, 2002, p. 78.

32. Quoted in Rebecca Wallwork, "Justin Timberlake."

33. Quoted in Tauber, et al., "Justin Timberlake."

34. Quoted in Margo Whitmire, "Timberlake's Appeal 'Justified' by Solo Success," *Billboard*, December 7, 2002, p. 22.

35. Quoted in Jenny Eliscu, "The New King of Pop," *Rolling Stone*, December 25, 2003, p. 44.

36. Quoted in "Justin," *Rolling Stone*, June 26, 2003, p. 50.

37. Quoted in Jenny Eliscu, "The New King of Pop."

38. Quoted in "Justin," *Rolling Stone*.

39. Quoted in Jenny Eliscu, "Justin Grows Up," *Rolling Stone*, May 18, 2006, p. 210.

40. Quoted in ABC News, "Justin on Britney: 'In Love From the Start.'"

Chapter Five: Branching Out Beyond Music

41. Quoted in Ken Barnes, "Music, Not Scandal, Is the Star," *USA Today*, February 9, 2004, p. 01d.

42. Quoted in Scaggs, "Justin Timberlake Revs Up His Sex Machine."

43. Quoted in Scaggs, "Justin Timberlake Revs Up His Sex Machine."

Chapter Six: New Directions

44. Quoted in Scaggs, "Justin Timberlake Revs Up His Sex Machine."

45. Quoted in Brian Hiatt, "Pop's New Hitmaker," *Rolling Stone*, October 5, 2006, p. 18.

46. Quoted in Scaggs, "Justin Timberlake Revs Up His Sex Machine."

47. Gavin Edwards, "Justin Timberlake," *Rolling Stone*, March 8, 2007, p. 98.

48. Quoted in Tim Stack, "Justified Acting Career?," *Entertainment Weekly*, April 28, 2006, p. 20.

49. Quoted in Stack, "Justified Acting Career?"

50. Quoted in Oliva Abel, et al., "Justin Through the Years," *People*, July 18, 2005, p. 26.

51. Quoted in Peter Travers, "The Social Network," *Rolling Stone*, October 14, 2010. www.rollingstone.com/movies/movie-reviews/the-social-network-113030/.

52. Jon Dolan, "The 20/20 Experience 2 of 2," *Rolling Stone*, September 30, 2013. www.rollingstone.com/music/music-album-reviews/the-20-20-experience-2-of-2-120677/.

53. Ryan Reed, "Justin Timberlake to Receive Songwriters Hall of Fame's 'Contemporary Icon' Award," *Rolling Stone*, May 8, 2019. www.rollingstone.com/music/music-news/justin-timberlake-songwriters-hall-of-fame-833022/.

54. Quoted in Reed, "Justin Timberlake to Receive Songwriters Hall of Fame's 'Contemporary Icon' Award."

Justin Timberlake Year by Year

1981

Justin Randall Timberlake is born on January 31 in Memphis, Tennessee.

1992

Timberlake makes his television debut as a contestant on *Star Search* but does not win.

1993

Timberlake is asked to join the cast of *The All New Mickey Mouse Club*.

1995

The musical group *NSYNC is formed with Timberlake, JC Chasez, Joey Fatone, Chris Kirkpatrick, and Lance Bass.

1997

*NSYNC's first album is released in Europe, and the group tours in Europe and Asia, as well as South Africa and Mexico.

1998

*NSYNC's debut album is released in the United States. Their holiday album, *Home for Christmas*, is released in November.

2000

*NSYNC's third album, *No Strings Attached*, is released and sets a record for selling 2.4 million copies in the first week of its release. Timberlake appears in the Disney Channel movie *Model Behavior*.

2001

*NSYNC's fourth album, *Celebrity*, is released. Timberlake contributes to the songwriting and production of a number of the album's tracks.

2002

Timberlake ends a three-and-a-half-year relationship with Britney Spears. In late fall, his first solo album, *Justified*, is released to critical acclaim.

2004

Timberlake's appearance in the Super Bowl halftime show with Janet Jackson causes a stir when he rips away part of her costume and reveals her breast. Timberlake wins two Grammy Awards, for "Cry Me a River" and *Justified.*

2006

FutureSex/LoveSounds, Timberlake's second solo album, is released and is well received.

2007

Timberlake wins two Grammy Awards, for "SexyBack" and "My Love." He stars in the film *Alpha Dog* and receives solid reviews for his acting. Timberlake and Jessica Biel start dating.

2010

The Social Network is released, starring Timberlake as Sean Parker. The movie receives rave reviews, and Timberlake's performance is praised.

2011

Biel and Timberlake end their relationship early in the year but get back together months later.

2012

Timberlake proposes marriage to Biel in Montana; the couple gets married in October.

2013

The 20/20 Experience parts one and two are released.

2015

Timberlake and Biel's son, Silas Randall, is born.

2016

Timberlake voices the character of Branch in *Trolls*.

2018

Timberlake's book, *Hindsight: & All the Things I Can't See in Front of Me,* is released; Timberlake performs at the Super Bowl; and *Man of the Woods* is released. Timberlake has to cancel a portion of the tour for the album because of bruised vocal cords.

2019

The Man of the Woods Tour resumes; Timberlake receives a Contemporary Icon award from the Songwriters Hall of Fame.

2020

Trolls World Tour is released, with Timberlake reprising the role of Branch.

For More Information

Books

Roach, Martin. *Justin Timberlake: The Unofficial Book*. London, UK: Virgin Books, 2003.

This photo-filled book aimed at his fans tracks Timberlake's career from his days with *The All New Mickey Mouse Club* to his success with *NSYNC and as a solo artist.

Schwartz, Heather E. *Justin Timberlake: From Mousketeer to Megastar*. Minneapolis, MN: Lerner Publications Company, 2015.

Schwartz's book has plenty of information on Justin Timberlake and full-color photos.

Smith, Sean. *Justin: The Unauthorized Biography*. London, UK: Simon & Schuster, 2004.

This easy read looks at Timberlake's music career and explores his personal relationships.

Timberlake, Justin. *Hindsight: & All the Things I Can't See in Front of Me*. New York, NY: HarperCollins, 2018.

This book features behind the scenes and private photos, as well as Timberlake's thoughts on fame, fatherhood, and being a husband.

Websites

Internet Movie Database
(www.imdb.com/name/nm0005493/maindetails)
This website offers photos, a brief biography of Justin Timberlake, and an updated list of his acting work.

Justin Timberlake
(www.justintimberlake.com)
Timberlake's website has videos as well as information on his music and tours.

Justin Timberlake on Facebook
(www.facebook.com/justintimberlake/)
The official Facebook page for Justin Timberlake has information on tours, photos, new music, and more.

Justin Timberlake on Instagram
(www.instagram.com/justintimberlake)
Justin Timberlake's Instagram has behind the scenes and personal photos.

Justin Timberlake on Twitter
(twitter.com/jtimberlake)
The official Twitter page of Justin Timberlake has up-to-date information on new music, movies, and tours.

Index

Picture Credits

Cover Tinseltown/Shutterstock.com; p. 8 Bob Berg/Getty Images; pp. 10–11 Kevin Mazur/WireImage/Getty Images; p. 12 David Crotty/Patrick McMullan via Getty Images; p. 15 Jeff Kravitz/FilmMagic/Getty Images; p. 17 ZUMA/Alamy Stock Photo; pp. 18–19 Buena Vista Television/Courtesy: Everett Collection; p. 22 Mark Weiss/WireImage/Getty Images; p. 25 Mike Prior/Getty Images; p. 28 Larry Busacca/WireImage/Getty Images; p. 30 Paul Natkin/Getty Images; p. 32 Steve Grayson/Online USA, Inc./Getty Images; p. 35 Featureflash Photo Agency/Shutterstock.com; pp. 37, 38–39, 64 KMazur/WireImage/Getty Images; p. 43 Jeffery Mayer/WireImage/Getty Images; p. 45 Greg Campbell/WireImage/Getty Images; p. 48 J. Shearer/WireImage/Getty Images; p. 51 Kathy Hutchins/Shutterstock.com; p. 55 Denise Truscello/WireImage/Getty Images; p. 57 George Pimentel/WireImage/Getty Images; pp. 60–61 M. Caulfield/WireImage/Getty Images; pp. 62–63 Kevin Kane/WireImage/Getty Images; p. 68 Lisa Blumenfeld/Getty Images; p. 71 Jeff Haynes/AFP/Getty Images; p. 72 J. Countess/WireImage/Getty Images; p. 74 Gareth Davies/Getty Images; p. 80 Steve Granitz/WireImage/Getty Images; p. 82 Todd Williamson/Getty Images; pp. 84–85 Kevin Winter/Getty Images for JT; pp. 86–87 Kevin Mazur/Getty Images for Live Nation.

About the Author

Nicole Horning has been a fan of Justin Timberlake's and *NSYNC's since the 1998 Disney Channel special. Before earning her bachelor's degree in English and master's degree in special education, she was a member of the *NSYNC fan club and attended every *NSYNC concert in her area. Today, she lives in Western New York with her cats, Khaleesi and Evie, and still screams like a preteen girl at Justin Timberlake concerts.